The Three Silly Ghosts Gruff

by Liza Charlesworth
illustrated by John Lund

ISBN: 979-8-225-02077-4

Publisher: Tara Welty
Creative Director: Tannaz Fassihi; Designer: Cynthia Ng

1 2 3 4 5 6 7 8 9 10 68 34 33 32 31 30 29 28 27 26 25

Made in Jiaxing City, China. First printing, August 2025.

SCHOLASTIC

This is the tale of three ghost brothers
named Benny, Kenny, and Lenny Gruff.
The Gruff ghosts had a fantastic life.
Each night, when the sky grew dark
and the moon rose high—zippity, zoom!
They flew outside to be scary.

"BOOOOOOOOOOOO!" yelled Benny.
"BOOOOOOOOOOOO!" yelled Kenny.
"BOOOOOOOOOOOO!" yelled Lenny.
There was just one itty-bitty problem:
The Gruff ghosts were silly, NOT scary.
"You three are so funny. You should do a comedy show!" said their pal Frank.

One day, the brothers spotted a poster for a huge party at the creepy castle. There was just one itty-bitty problem: You had to be very scary to get in. So, the Gruff ghosts flew home and took turns making lots and lots of spooky faces. "Nice work. We got this!" said Lenny.

By and by, the sky grew dark and
the moon rose high. Zippity, zoom!
The Gruff ghosts flew to the party.
There was just one itty-bitty problem:
To get to the creepy castle, they needed
to cross a bridge over a moat. On the bridge
stood a green witch by the name of Willa.
And Willa got to decide who went inside.

The Gruff ghosts hid behind a tree and peeked at all the creatures trying to go to the party. A tall, white skeleton crept up to the bridge. "Very scary!" said Willa and she let him in. Next came Frank and a wrapped-up mummy. "Very scary and very, very scary!" said Willa. She let them both cross the bridge and go in.

“I think we are just as scary as those three,”
said Benny with a grin. “I will go first.”
Zippity, zoom! He flew over to the bridge.
Then he made a face and yelled, “BOOOO!”
What did Willa do? Well, she just giggled.
“Nice try, Benny, but not scary,” she said.
“I’m sad to say I cannot let you in.”

So, Benny went back to his two brothers and said, “No luck! Willa didn’t let me in.”
“Darn!” said Kenny. “Time for me to try.”
Zippity, zoom! He flew over to the bridge.
He flipped upside-down and yelled, “BOOOO!”
Did Willa feel fear? Nope. She just giggled.
“Hee-hee, Kenny. Not a bit scary,” she said.
“I simply cannot let you go in.”

So, Kenny went back to his two brothers and told them the sad news: “She said NO.” “Drat,” said Lenny. “That means it’s my turn.” Zippity, zoom! He flew over to the bridge. He puffed himself up and yelled, “BOOOO!” Did Willa shudder? Nope. But she did giggle. “Lenny, you are way more funny than scary. Sorry, pal. I cannot let you go in.”

So, Lenny went back to his two brothers and cried,
“BOO-HOO! BOO-HOO! I feel bad. I failed, too!”
“Well, failure is not an option,” said Benny.
“Yes,” agreed Kenny. “We need a new plan.”
Then Lenny said, “Wait. I think I’ve got it!
If we all fly over to the bridge TOGETHER,
we will be three times as scary. . .
and Willa will HAVE to let us in.”

So it was decided. The three Gruff ghosts flew over to the bridge and worked as a team.
Benny whirled around in a big circle.
Kenny wrinkled his nose and scowled.
Lenny turned a spooky shade of blue.
Then they all screamed a long, loud "BOOOOOOOOOOOOOOOOOOOOOOO!"

Did Willa the witch shake and quake? Yes, she did. Then she began to giggle and chuckle and cackle and howl and chortle and snicker so hard. . . she slipped right off that bridge and fell into the moat. SPLISH, SPLASH!

What did the three silly ghosts do to help?
They reached down into the moat with Willa's broom and told her to grab it.
Then, quick as a wink, they tugged her out.
She was dripping wet, but safe and sound.
"Thank you for saving my life," said Willa.
"I will let all three of you go to the party."

“Yippee, skippy!” screamed Benny and Kenny. “But WHY are you letting us go?” asked Lenny. “Well,” replied Willa with a smile, “the three of you made me giggle so hard, I fell off a bridge. And we DO need a good comedy show tonight. Will the three silly ghosts Gruff take the stage?” “Yes, indeed!” said Benny, Kenny, and Lenny.

Inside the castle, the party was jumping.
Benny gobbled snacks with the skeleton.
Kenny played games with the mummy.
Lenny chatted with their old pal, Frank.
Then they all boogied and oogied until. . .

BING-BONG! The clock struck midnight. Zippity, zoom! Benny, Kenny, and Lenny hopped on the stage to do a comedy show. They told tales. They made spooky faces and screamed a long, loud "BOOOOOOOOOO!" Were the three silly ghosts Gruff very scary? Nope! But they were very, very, very funny!